MAR 2013

DEAR FLYARY

Written by Dianne Young

Illustrated by John Martz

Kids Can Press

For the Robins and the Story Refiners — good friends who write — D.Y.

For Mom and Dad, for making sure I always had access to books and drawing supplies — J.M.

Text © 2012 Dianne Young
Illustrations © 2012 John Martz

Kids Can Press acknowledges the financial support of the Government of Ontario, through the Ontario Media Development Corporation's Ontario Book Initiative; the Ontario Arts Council; the Canada Council for the Arts; and the Government of Canada, through the BPIDP, for our publishing activity.

Published in Canada by
Kids Can Press Ltd.
25 Dockside Drive
Toronto, ON M5A 0B5

Published in the U.S. by
Kids Can Press Ltd.
2250 Military Road
Tonawanda, NY 14150

www.kidscanpress.com

The artwork in this book was rendered in Photoshop.
The text is set in Vag Rounded.

Edited by Yvette Ghione
Designed by Marie Bartholomew

This book is smyth sewn casebound.
Manufactured in Tseung Kwan O, NT Hong Kong, China, in 10/2011 by Paramount Printing Co. Ltd.

CM 12 0 9 8 7 6 5 4 3 2 1

Library and Archives Canada Cataloguing in Publication

Young, Dianne, 1959–
        Dear Flyary / written by Dianne Young ; illustrated by John Martz.

ISBN 978-1-55453-448-7

I. Martz, John, 1978– II. Title.

PS8597.O5923D43 2012   jC813'.54   C2011-904468-4

Kids Can Press is a **ʕ●rʊs**™ Entertainment company

THIS BOOK BELONGS TO

GOBY   FRAZZLE PATTZER

LOCATOR   61325 GLANK QUADRANT

MERFATIL 058Δ

BEAM   9637P45

DROPDAY   76 RED MOON 4826

75 Red Moon 4851

Dear Flyary,

Oldpop gave you to me for my dropday. He wants me to scrib down everything about my first spaceship. It's a Pattzer keepition. He even showed me the drivary that his oldpop (my real-real-oldpop) scribbed. It was pretty laffy.

76 Red Moon 4851

Dear Flyary,

Gladdy dropday to me! Finally — old enough to have my own spaceship! First thing this waker, I went out and bought a brand new Model 7. You should see it! It's bright red with white racing stripes down the sides and jet-black thrusters. It's flixsome!

HUM·M·M HUM·M·M HUM·M·M
HUM·M·M HUM·M·M HUM·M·M

77 Red Moon 4851

Dear Flyary,

I took a spin to Harbatil today, just to hear the engine run.
What a spaceship! It purrs like a tarkelby.

Just wait till everyone at the Binkler Factory sees me fly up
in this! They'll be tan with envy.

78 Red Moon 4851

Dear Flyary,

Everyone bighearts my new spaceship! Even my boss, Tur Labbit, said, "Nice ship, Fizzle." (He always gets my goby wrong.)

Dear Flyary,

What a day! I was on my way to the greeball game (the Binklers were playing the Jifflers) when my viewtiful red spaceship started making a strange noise! It wasn't a loud noise, though. I had to listen with all four of my ears just to hear it.

Luckily, I peepered a small repair station just off the flyway.
"Wurpitz Hoolo's Spaceship Repair, Wash and Fillerup Station,"
the sign said in a friendly voice. I headed straight there.

Wurpitz checked the engine over thoroughly. "It's okay, Frazzle,"
she told me at last, wiping her hands on her hoveralls. "It's just
a tiny hole in the flyjacker. Happens all the time.
I wouldn't even bother fixing it if I were you.
You'll get used to the noise."

What a relief!

And to top it off, the Binklers beat the Jifflers purple to gold.
A giddy day after all.

Dear Flyary,

Wurpitz was right about the noise — I kind of smallheart
it now.

HUM · PIFFLE · PIFFLE · HUM · M · M
HUM · PIFFLE · PIFFLE · HUM · M · M

Dear Flyary,

Gladdy decathird dropday to me! Today I got to choose my first noteymaker. I couldn't decide if I wanted a snilkum or a snoogle, but then I saw a snilkum the same bright red as my spaceship! I can hardly wait to learn to play it.

My co-jobber Nithrak (we call him Nega-rak) thinks I should have gotten an upfit for my spaceship instead of a noteymaker. He read in *Sharp Ship* that some Model 7s were prone to making weird noises.

"So are noteymakers!" I said.

But then he said, "Yes, but noteymakers don't exboom!"

Dear Flyary,

You won't believe what happened this after-waker! I was on my way home from the factory when my little red spaceship started making another strange noise! This noise was a bit louder than the last one — I could hear it with just three of my ears.

HUM · PIFFLE · PIFFLE HUM · TICK · TICK
HUM · PIFFLE · PIFFLE HUM · TICK · TICK

I was scared (Nithrak had made me wervous), but at least I knew what to do. I flew straight to Wurpitz Hoolo's Spaceship Repair, Wash and Fillerup Station.

Wurpitz checked the engine carefully. "Relax, Frazzle," she told me, wiping her noses with her hanky. "It's just a sticky megalad. Quite common in the Model 7. No need for repairs. It won't exboom. And you'll get used to the noise."

Thank giddiness! Or I guess I should say, thank Wurpitz!

Dear Flyary,

Wurpitz was right again about the noise — it's actually pretty koof.

HUM·PIFFLE·PIFFLE HUM·TICK·TICK
HUM·PIFFLE·PIFFLE HUM·TICK·TICK

76 Red Moon 4859

Gladdy dropday to me! I could have bought a new spaceship today. My best friend, Bizzle, thinks I should have. The Model 8s are out now, and he said they come in koof new colors like rugger, blanny and nori. (I didn't have the heart to tell him that those are just the Harbat words for red, white and black.) But I still bigheart my little "rugger" Model 7 with its "blanny" stripes and "nori" thrusters. (They do sound koof!) Maybe next perkin.

Dear Flyary,

Maybe Bizzle was right! I was on my way to the Flamper's Day Parade (I smallheart the spinblasters the best, don't you?) when my giddy old spaceship started making another strange noise! It was quite a bit louder than the last one — I could hear it with just two of my ears.

I flew right to Wurpitz's, but of course it was closed for Flamper's Day! I was too wervous to keep flying it (garn that Nithrak anyway), so I beamed Bizzle and he picked me up in his new Model 8. His dome is nearish, so I spent the pre-waker at his place. We missed the parade but watched the redo on the seebox. The spinblasters were still flixsome!

This waker Bizzle flew me back to Wurpitz's, but I had to listen to him blah-blah on about the Model 8 and how it was time I traded in my old Model 7. I finally told him my ship was like an old friend, and I don't mind if old friends are a bit blustrating sometimes. (I don't think he caught on.)

By the time I got there, Wurpitz had already had a look at the engine. "Don't worry, Frazzle," she told me, adjusting her greeball cap. "It's just a loose tarsnaggle. Not surprising in a ship this old, even one as well cared for as yours. Hardly worth fixing. You'll get used to the noise. And, no, it won't exboom."

Whew! I thought for sure it would be something non-giddious this time.

Dear Flyary,

I bigheart my giddy old spaceship — my friend.

BOINK· PIFFLE·PIFFLE *HUM*·TICK·TICK
BOINK· PIFFLE·PIFFLE *HUM*·TICK·TICK

Dear Flyary,

My poor old spaceship! Not even a perkin since the last time. I was on my way home from my snilkum lesson (I'm getting pretty giddy — you should hear me wail on "What's New, Tarkelby?") when my spaceship made one very loud noise. It was so loud I could have heard it using none of my ears at all!

CLUNK!

That was it. (At least it didn't exboom!) But there I was, stuck in the middle of the flyway. I couldn't go up. I couldn't go down. I just couldn't go. What a kurpitch! I'd never hear the end of it if Nithrak and Bizzle ever found out.

I speed-beamed Wurpitz's, but it was already closed for the pre-waker. I just couldn't beam Bizzle, so I took a fetchmi home instead. I'll beam Wurpitz first thing in the waker.

This waker Wurpitz sent a towship to pick me up and haul my spaceship in off the flyway.

Wurpitz took one look at the engine, shook her head and said, "Sorry, Frazzle. The engine can't be fixed. We'll just have to replace it."

So while I paced in the sitter room, Wurpitz disintegrated the old engine and fabricated a new one.

"There you go, Frazzle," she said when she was done (it only took a few glartons). "Giddy as new. That'll be 92 megasopps, please."

I was so relieved I gave her a woppasopp and told her to keep the change. I could hardly wait to try out my giddy old spaceship with the brand new engine. So off I flew.

HUM·M·M HUM·M·M HUM·M·M
HUM·M·M HUM·M·M HUM·M·M

Whoa! *Hummm?* I turned around and flurried back to the station. "Wurpitz! Wurpitz!" I callered.

"Hey, Frazzle," said Wurpitz, casually strolling over as if everything was dunky-dory. "What's the matter?"

"There's something wrong with this engine! Listen!"

HUM·M·M
HUM·M·M
HUM·M·M

It almost looked like Wurpitz smiled! (Can you believe it?) "I think I know what the problem is, Frazzle. Your new engine just needs a few minor adjustments. Come with me."

"See here?" she asked, as she pointed to the engine. "This flyjacker has no flow-through port," and she pulled out a long needle and poked a tiny hole in it.

Poke!

"And look," she continued, "this megalad is much too slippery." She pulled out a bottle of Space-Goo and glorped a little on it.

"And finally," she said (and I'm sure I saw her smile this time), "this tarsnaggle is way too tight," and she pulled out her scrench and loosened it just a tad.

"Give it a fly," she told me, as she slid her peekers up on top of her head. "I'm sure you'll be gladdier with it now."

And I was. In fact, I was so gladdy I left there grinning from ear to ear to ear to ear.

That Wurpitz is so wise.

BOINK· PIFFLE·PIFFLE HUM·TICK·TICK
BOINK· PIFFLE·PIFFLE HUM·TICK·TICK